Hellooooooo!

My name's **TY**, and I'm seven.

But you might already **KNOW** that. If you didn't, now you do!

This book that you are holding is all about **ME**. It's my third book about my **crazy, hectic** life.

It's filled with **classmates** and **best friends** and lots of **sisters**, too.

And maybe even a **BIRD CHASE**! Okay, *probably* a bird chase.

But if you want to hear all about it, you have to start reading. **NOW**!

THE LIFE OF TY

Friends of a Feather

BOOK 3

LAUREN
MYRACLE

Illustrated by Jed Henry

PUFFIN BOOKS

For Rosanne Lauer, who makes books better-er

PUFFIN BOOKS
An imprint of Penguin Random House LLC
375 Hudson Street
New York, New York 10014

First published in the United States of America by Dutton Children's Books,
an imprint of Penguin Group (USA) LLC, 2015
Published by Puffin Books, an imprint of Penguin Random House LLC, 2015

Text copyright © 2015 by Lauren Myracle
Illustrations copyright © 2015 by Jed Henry

CIP Data is available.

Puffin Books ISBN 978-0-14-242320-2

Printed in the United States of America

Designed by Irene Vandervoort

1 3 5 7 9 10 8 6 4 2

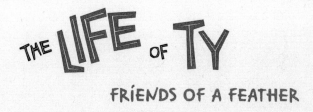

THE LIFE OF TY

FRIENDS OF A FEATHER

BOOK 3

CHAPTER ONE

I am bouncy bouncy bouncy in the backseat of the car. My best friend Joseph is finally out of the hospital, *and today he's coming back to school*!

Joseph had leukemia, which is a bad sickness and worse than a cold, but now he's better.

I've been missing him for*ever*, but now he'll be back in Mrs. Webber's class with me. Second grade will go back to normal. Ty and Joseph, Joseph and Ty, just like the old days. And I won't have to play with Lexie anymore, who Mom says is a "challenge." Or Taylor, who sometimes kicks!

Well, I might play with them sometimes, but I won't be stuck with them. It'll be my choice. With Joseph back at school, Lexie and Taylor and everyone else will be like the wiggly lime Jell-O at Morrison's, which is a restaurant where you go through a food line and pick whatever you want, including your own dessert.

If I'm in the mood for lime Jell-O, then fine. But if I'm in the mood for chocolate pudding, which I pretty much always am, then too bad for the lime Jell-O and hurray for the chocolate pudding, because the chocolate pudding's name is Joseph. *Yippee!*

I giggle, and my sister Winnie looks back at me. Winnie is my middle-est sister. She's sitting next to Sandra, who is my oldest sister. Sandra's the one driving. My youngest sister is at home trying to eat her toes; her name is Teensy Baby Maggie.

"You have such a cute giggle," Winnie says. "Are you happy about Joseph? Is that what you're thinking about?"

"Remember in kindergarten, when Joseph was too scared of Sandra to say her name?" I ask. "But we spied on her anyway, and Joseph screamed when she spotted us?"

"Oh yeah!" Winnie says. "Sandra was just 'The Big One'!" Winnie widens her eyes and pretends to be Joseph. *"Oh no, The Big One's coming! Oh no, The Big One saw us!"*

Sandra *hmmph*s. She takes a left into Trinity's parking lot and gets in the drop-off lane.

"Joseph isn't afraid of *me*, though," Winnie goes on. She taps her chin. "He *loooooves* me, because I am the nicer sister. And sweeter and smarter and more fun to look at."

"More fun to look at?" Sandra says. "Like how a severed foot is fun to look at? Is that what you mean?"

"Ew, and no," Winnie says.

Sandra winks at me. Yesterday she showed me a picture of a severed foot on her phone. A *real live* severed foot. It was from a man in a motorcycle accident who'd been wearing sneakers instead of motorcycle boots. When his body skidded down the highway, *sloosh*, off came his foot.

The picture was interesting, but I wasn't sure how long I should look at it, or if I should look at it at all. Sandra told me not to worry. She said the motorcycle man posted the picture himself because he wanted other people to remember to wear motorcycle boots.

"He didn't think he'd be in an accident that day, but he was," Sandra said. "Expect the unexpected, buddy. That's the life lesson here."

I like the life lessons Sandra tells me. Sandra *and* Winnie. I'm glad I have older sisters to tell me how the world works, because sometimes it's confusing. I'm glad I have a baby sister, too. I'll get to tell her how the world works, once she learns to talk.

Also, a while back I promised to get Maggie a pet, and I need to be a man of my word, even if Maggie doesn't know words yet.

Yikes, I need to get Baby Maggie a pet!

Which makes me wonder something, which I ask Winnie and Sandra.

"Do you think Joseph still has Sneaky Bob Lizard?"

"Probably," Winnie says.

Sandra inches the car forward. It's pretty much impossible to have a wreck in the drop-off lane, so I unbuckle my seat belt and scoot forward. "Do you think he's still fuzzy-headed?"

"Joseph or Sneaky Bob Lizard?" Sandra says.

"Ha-ha. Do you think he remembers all the kids in our class?"

"Unless someone clonked him on the head," Winnie says. "He missed . . . what? Six months of school? Of course he remembers the kids in your class."

I knew that already, actually. I just wanted to hear it. I know the answer to my next question, too, but I ask it anyway. "Do you think he remembers *me*?"

Winnie snorts. "No, Ty, he forgot you. He also forgot spying on Sandra, making pants out of duct tape—"

"And vests and swords," Sandra says.

"And those horrible drinks you dared each other to drink!" Winnie exclaims. "I'm *sure* he forgot those."

I smile. We used ketchup and yucky mustard and lemon curd, and milk and soy sauce and orange juice. Oh, and Cheez Whiz. I don't think either of us will forget those drinks, ever.

Joseph and I made those drinks last fall. Now it's spring. We can still do spying and duct tape and yucky drinks, but we can also go outside and drop Mentos into bottles of Coke, which'll make the Coke spray up and soak everybody. We'll just have to make sure Mom is busy with Teensy Baby Maggie.

Teensy Baby Maggie! My eyeballs nearly pop out. *I* know Teensy Baby Maggie—of course I do, she's my sister—but Joseph has never met her.

That is so weird!

The car in front of us drives off. Sandra pulls into the space where kids are supposed to get out, then slams on the brakes. *Really* slams them, because she knows I like it when she makes the car rock back and forth.

"Move your booty, mister," she says.

I scramble out, slinging my backpack over my shoulder.

Winnie leans over Sandra's lap. "Tell Joseph 'hi' for us, and that we're so glad he's back."

Sandra shoves Winnie off of her. "*If* he remembers you. If he doesn't, don't bother."

I laugh. Then I stop. I put my hand on the rubbery bit of Sandra's open window and say, "Hold on. What do you mean, *if* he remembers?"

"You said it, not me," Sandra says.

"Sandra, don't be mean," Winnie says.

Sandra shrugs. "Well, how do we know he *didn't* get clonked on the head?"

"He didn't," Winnie says.

"Maybe aliens took over his body, or he randomly got a brain transfer."

Winnie rolls her eyes. "No."

Sandra wags her finger. "Now, now. Remember what Mom says: The only thing you can be certain of in life is change."

My stomach clenches, because Mom does say that. Not every second, but yes. What if Joseph *doesn't* remember me?

Except he will. Joseph not remembering me would be like . . . like the earth turning upside-down. We'd all fall off and go floating into space.

"Sandra's just trying to provoke you, Ty," Winnie says. "Don't let her rain on your parade."

"What parade?" I say.

Sandra laughs and slaps the steering wheel. "Exactly."

She peels off, and I try to remember what "provoke" means. Something about a pin? About poking another person with a pin?

From the end of the drop-off lane, Sandra's last bit of advice floats back to me. "Expect the unexpected! The Big One always knows best!"

Expect the unexpected. I push and prod that thought in my mind as I trudge up the school's front stairs. It made sense with the motorcycle man and his decapitated foot (which might not be the right word, but I always forget the real one). I don't like it when it has to do with Joseph, though. With Joseph, I don't want to expect the unexpected.

Only Joseph didn't expect to get sick, did he? Just like the motorcycle man didn't expect to be in an accident?

But how can anyone expect the unexpected? It's like saying, "Tie your shoe, but without tying your shoe." Or telling a dog to turn into a cat, or marching over to the kitchen sink and ordering it to fly. Sinks *can't* fly! That's why they're called *sinks*!

Oh, fudge nickels, I think, walking faster. *Just go to Joseph. Duh.* Once I'm with Joseph, everything

will be fine. The earth won't turn upside-down
and no one will go floating into space. Duh!

"Ty!" someone calls.

I stop.

"Ty, help us!" the person says, and it's a girl,
and I'm pretty sure it's Hannah, who's in Mrs.
Webber's class with me. "You're our only hope!"

I turn, and yep, it's Hannah. She and Claire
have their backs pressed against the wall. They're
clinging to each other and trying to be shorter
and smaller than they really are. They're also gig-
gling. Taylor, who is a boy-Taylor, is standing in
front of them with his feet apart and his arms
spread wide.

"*Mwa-HA-ha-ha!*" he says. "Nobody can help
you, fools!"

"Yeah-huh, because Ty will," Hannah says.
"Hurry, Ty!"

I push my fingers against my forehead. This is
not how the morning is supposed to go, because:

A: I'm not supposed to have to deal with Taylor anymore, not unless I choose to. He's supposed to be the lime Jell-O.

B: Taylor is also using a maniac voice, but he's doing it wrong. It's *MWA-ha-ha*, not *mwa-HA-ha-ha*. What maniac says *mwa-HA-ha-ha*?

And, C: The waistband of Taylor's jeans is lower than his underwear, and I think letting the whole world see your underwear is a bad idea.

"Taylor, let them go," I say.

"Nope," Taylor says, popping the *p* sound.

To Hannah and Claire, I say, "Just walk around him."

"We can't," Hannah says. "He pooted!"

"He pooted, and we are gagging!" Claire says. She puts her hands to her throat. "Make"—gag—"him"—gag gag—"get out of here!"

I sigh. Taylor poots a lot, and his poots are stinkier than anyone's in the entire school. Like, you can walk into the art room and know that

Taylor was just there, because even when Taylor leaves, his poot-smell stays and stays.

I glance toward Mrs. Webber's room. Joseph is probably wondering where I am. I *could* abandon the girls and go to him. Only abandoning the girls would make my stomach hurt.

"Taylor, move," I tell him.

"Ooo-eee! Makin' bacon!" he says, squatting down. He holds his fists in by his sides and shakes his booty.

I suck in a big breath of air, take two giant steps forward, and grab Taylor around the waist. I tug. His booty comes toward me, but his feet stay planted where they are.

Then—*pbbbbbbbbb.* A cloud of stench glomps on to me. I sputter and flail, trying to get it off.

"See?" Hannah says.

My eyes water as I stumble backward. Pulling him didn't work, so what now?

A crane lift?

A superpower magnet like the ones at junk-yards that hold up entire cars?

A giant pair of very strong pliers that I could grab his belt loop with?

Or . . .

OR . . .

"Hannah, do you have gymnastics today?" I ask.

"Why?" Hannah says.

I wait. I push my eyeballs at her. I push them harder, and finally she gets it.

"Ohhhh," she says. "Why, yes, Ty. I *do* have gym-

nastics, and guess what? I even brought my leotard. My shiny pink leotard. If you want to go get it, it's in my cubby."

"Your gymnastics leotard? No!" Taylor says. His *ha-ha* face turns into a scared face. "Anything but that!"

"Let the girls go," I say. "Or I will get Hannah's pink shiny gymnastics leotard, and I'll bring it out here, and—"

"Okay!" he shouts. "You win, you win!" He flees down the hall toward the art room, and Hannah and Claire collapse with crazy laughing.

"Why is he scared of your gymnastics leotard?" Claire asks Hannah.

"I have no idea!" Hannah says.

I do. I know why. It's because sometimes Hannah changes into her leotard at the end of school, and everyone sees her in it. And sometimes her underwear peeks out, kind of. Which Taylor shouldn't be afraid of since people can see his underwear, too! Sheesh!

Hannah's laughter trickles off. "What's wrong, Ty? You look mad."

"I'm not," I say. But maybe I am, because I just realized something. Taylor pulled an unexpectedness on me by being here and bothering the girls right when I walked by. Then I turned around and pulled an unexpectedness on him, by bringing up Hannah's leotard.

My brain buzzes, and I sway.

Hannah rushes over and grabs me. "Ty?"

"Whoa," I say.

"You're probably light-headed," Claire says. "Probably because of Taylor's poots."

Hannah looks worried. "Do you want me to take you to the office?"

I shake free and head for Mrs. Webber's room. "No, I'm fine. I just got dizzy for a second."

Either that or the world *has* turned upside-down. Which if it did, I'm not fine at all.

CHAPTER TWO

oseph!" I call when I see him.

He turns at my voice. He's surrounded by other kids, and his face is shining and happy, and my first thought is that he is the sun, because he's at the center of things. He's the sun, and the kids gathered around him are the planets and stars and space junk and stuff.

My second thought is that he must be embarrassed of his hair, because he's wearing his red woolly hat, which is the same hat he wore last fall when he got sick. He was absent a lot to go get treatments, and the treatments made him bald.

My third thought is, *So?* Because when he got put in the hospital for real, Mom took me to visit

him almost every week, and I saw his bald head then. I thought he looked cool. And as he got better, and his hair started growing back, I saw his *fuzzy* head. I thought he looked cool then, too.

"Ty!" he calls back to me. His smile makes him light up even more.

I grin and hurry toward him, but I stop before I fully reach him. I'm not sure why. I know I'm still grinning, because my cheeks are tight, but for a second it's more of a frozen grin than a real grin.

It's strange. Joseph is finally back, and for some reason I feel shy.

I push harder on my smile and tell my legs to move.

"Out of the way, people!" I say to the kids circled around him. John makes room, and so does Chase. But Lexie, who was my loaner best friend while Joseph was gone, edges closer to Joseph instead of farther away.

"You're really here!" I say to Joseph.

"I know!" Joseph says back. "So are you!"

That makes me laugh, and my shyness melts away. Joseph is still Joseph, and I'm still me. He's wearing a shirt I've never seen before, but that's the only unexpectedness.

"*I* gave him that," Lexie says, as if she grew mind-reading powers when I wasn't watching. "My mom took me to visit him last night, and I gave him that shirt to say 'welcome back.'"

"Oh," I say. I take a longer look. Joseph's shirt, which Lexie gave him, has an octopus on it with a big head and googly eyes. The octopus's arms have suckers on them that make me think *ploop ploop ploop*.

For a shirt, it's sort of pretty awesome, and I'm jealous that Lexie was the one who gave it to him. I wish it was a babyish shirt instead, or dumb, so that later Joseph could tell me his mom made him wear it. Except no, because that would be like saying I wished Joseph's shirt was dumb. That I wanted Joseph, my best friend, to be wearing a dumb shirt.

Lexie smirks, and I imagine a cartoon picture of the octopus going *ploop ploop ploop* all over her head. There could be a speech bubble that showed her saying, *"OH NO, OCTOPUS POOP!"*

I grab Joseph's arm. "Did Mrs. Webber tell you where to sit yet?" I ask. "Let's ask if you can be by me."

"Too late," Chase says. He points to the desk next to his. Joseph's stuff is on top of it, including his backpack with the broken strap that he and I fixed with a rubber band.

I pull Joseph toward Mrs. Webber anyway.

"Mrs. Webber, can Joseph please be in Crazy Crabs?" I ask. The desks are set up in clusters all over the room, and each cluster has a name. Crazy Crabs, Super Sea Horses, Dapper Dolphins—like that, for all eight clusters. All the names have to do with the ocean because . . . well, I don't know why. But, huh . . . is that the reason Lexie gave him an octopus shirt?

"Or he could sit with me," Lexie says, elbowing her way in.

"No, because we don't have an octopus group," I say. "We have Jiggling Jellyfish, but no octopuses."

Lexie looks at me funny. "Octo*pi*," she says. She turns back to Mrs. Webber. "There's tons of room by me and Breezie, and we'll take good care of him. Right, Breezie?"

Breezie is Lexie's real best friend. I scan the room, wanting to know what *she* thinks of this idea.

"Uh-huh," Breezie says. She's in the beanbag chair in the reading nook, her knees pulled to her chest and her arms wrapped around her shins. She's staring at the floor.

"We should let Joseph decide," I say. "Joseph, whose group do you want to be in?"

"If you stay in Wonderful Whales, you'll be closer to Lester," Chase says, because suddenly he's there, too.

"Who's Lester?" Joseph asks.

"Our class snake," Chase says. He tilts his head, like how could Joseph forget Lester?

And I think, *Because Joseph wasn't here when we got Lester, that's how.* Chase would know that if he were Joseph's best friend. But he isn't, so he should stay out of it.

"I'll show you Lester after we move your stuff," I say.

"Or I will," Lexie says.

"Or I will, because you already have a desk, and it's next to mine," Chase says.

Taylor bursts into the room. "Ooo-eee!" he says. He sticks out his booty and pulls his fists in at his sides, just like he did with Hannah and Claire. "Makin' bacon!"

I scowl at him, because this is all his fault. Everything that's making me feel . . . twisty-uppy is Taylor's fault. If he hadn't ambushed Hannah and Claire with his poot smell, then I would have gotten to Mrs. Webber's room earlier.

If I'd gotten to Mrs. Webber's room earlier, then I'd have been with Joseph when Mrs. Webber assigned him a desk, and I'd have made sure he was a Crazy Crab.

"OOO-EEE!" Taylor says, even louder. "MAKIN'—"

"Taylor, no," Mrs. Webber interrupts. "No more bacon, any of you," which is unfair because no one was making bacon except Taylor.

Taylor says, *Mwa-HA-ha-ha!* and Mrs. Webber says, "Taylor? Enough!"

Her voice is sharp. Joseph flinches.

"Oh, Joseph," Mrs. Webber says, softening her tone. She squeezes his shoulder, and he looks at her hand. She lets go.

"Right," she says, going back to teacher mode. "Put away your free-choice activities, everyone. It's time to work on your vocabulary sheet."

My heart flutters. "But—"

"We'll figure out the desk situation later."

"But Mrs. Webber—"

"It's okay," Joseph says. "I don't mind."

Lexie smiles triumphantly. "Yeah, *Ty*," she says. "He doesn't *mind*."

A lump forms in my throat.

"Wait," Joseph says. "I *do* mind, but I don't . . . you know . . ."

It seems like everybody is silent at the same time, and my twisty-uppy feelings get twisty-uppier. I'm blushing. I can feel it.

Then kids start talking and moving and tidying up the free-choice stations. Joseph tries to get me to look at him, which I know because we're so good at feeling each other's eyeball lasers. I don't meet his gaze, though. I don't know why for sure. It's more than Joseph being a Wonderful Whale, but I can't exactly say how.

I sit down, open my desk, and take out my pen with the four different colors: red, blue, green, and black. It's an excellent pen. It's a lot cooler than a pretend octopus. All I have to do is decide which color I want and click the clicky thing. Then, *cha-chink*! Out pops whichever color I choose.

I click the clicky green thing, and *cha-chink*, the green ink tip comes out. I click the red thing, and *cha-chink*, the red ink tip comes out. I *hmph* under my breath. At least my pen works.

I open my notebook to a clean page and draw Cyber Grape. He's supposed to be purple, but I draw him using blue. I invented him, so I can do whatever I want. Only he looks weird blue, so I open my desk again, thinking I'll trade in my four-color pen for a purple marker.

I do the switch and close my desk, but now I feel bad for my four-color pen. It's not fair to make my four-color pen go, *Yay! I'm coming out of the desk! I'm going to be used!* just to put it away and make it go, *Wh-what? No! Don't close the desk! Don't close the de-s-s-s-s-s-s-s-k!*

But Cyber Grape is a grape, and not the green

sort of grape but the purple sort of grape. And yes, I invented him, but he looks *weird* blue.

He.

Is.

Supposed.

To.

Be.

PURPLE.

"Ty? Are you working on vocabulary?" Mrs. Webber asks.

"Yes, ma'am," I say, because I kind of am. I will in a second, but no one is doing their vocabulary sheet yet.

I think about things. I drum my fingers on top of my desk. Then I give a quick nod. I open my desk and take my four-color pen back out. I put my four-color pen next to my purple marker, and I say, "Just hold on, okay? You'll get a turn, too."

I say this to the pen. I say it in my head.

I flip to the next page in my notebook. With

the purple marker, I draw Cyber Grape. I draw him standing on top of the world, which is Earth, and which I draw with my four-color pen since Earth is green and blue when you're looking at it from outer space.

I draw more quickly. I'm on a roll. I draw all the planets, even Pluto, because I don't think it's fair to say out of nowhere that *Ha-ha, Pluto, you're not a planet anymore.*

I draw the planets out of order, though. I scatter them over the page like a handful of Skittles, with Mars in the top right corner and Saturn off to the left and Neptune squished beneath Pluto. I make Jupiter the smallest planet of all, even though I'm not dumb and I know it's actually the biggest.

I add stars and asteroids and space junk, which is a real thing and not something I made up. Space junk is made up of busted-up satellites, pieces of rockets that are floating around in space, and rocks that aren't big enough to be asteroids. They'll float around in space forever, unless they break through the atmosphere and burn up or turn into meteors.

Except space junk is a lonely thing to think about. It makes Cyber Grape lonely, too, and I don't know why I stuck him up in space or why I drew this stupid picture in the first place.

I rip it out of my notebook and crumple it up. Then I rip out my first picture, the wrong one of Cyber Grape being blue, and crumple *that* one up.

Lots of kids still haven't settled down, and Breezie is the only person doing her vocabulary sheet. Mrs. Webber claps her hands and tells everyone to go to their seats. When they don't, she flashes the classroom light off and on. Finally people jump to it, because the next step after flashing the lights is time-out. If you get a time-out, you have to sit in the hall or sometimes on the floor in another teacher's classroom. Nobody wants that.

Elizabeth steers John over to my cluster of desks.

"Sit," she commands, pressing down on his shoulders.

He drops into his seat, and Elizabeth goes to collect her next person. Elizabeth likes telling people to do things.

"Hi, Ty," John says.

"Hi," I say. I shove my wadded-up drawings into my desk.

"I have a loose tooth," he says. "Want to see?"

"No," I say. "And just to warn you, it might not really be loose. It might be a fake out."

"It might?"

I nod, because that very thing happened to me. Two weeks ago, Taylor whacked me on the playground and made my tooth loose, but a few days later, my gums sucked themselves back around it and suddenly it wasn't loose anymore.

Loose teeth becoming un-loose. Another

thing that's not supposed to happen, but that sometimes happens anyway.

John doesn't reply. I peek at him, and his expression makes me feel bad, because it's possible I made *him* feel bad. I peek at Joseph, using my hair to cover as much of my eyes as I can. His expression makes me feel bad, too, but in a different way. Joseph is talking to Chase as Elizabeth steers the two of them toward their seats. His eyes are happy, and his face is lit up like it was earlier.

Chase laughs, and so does Elizabeth, and so do Silas and Natalia, who haven't gone to their seats yet.

The four of them crowd around Joseph when he sits down. They breathe up his air molecules. Elizabeth should make Silas and Natalia go to their own desk cluster. She should make herself go to her own desk cluster.

She doesn't, and everyone talks and laughs.

Joseph is the sun, Chase and Elizabeth are planets, and I'm space junk.

I put my arms on my desk and my head on my arms.

I want the universe to line up right again.

CHAPTER THREE

The next morning at breakfast, Winnie asks me what's wrong.

"Nothing," I say. "Or . . . I don't know. Maybe something." I shrug and push my eggs around with my fork. They're a shade of yellow that usually makes me happy, but not today. Today my stomach is too worried for eggs.

"Is it Joseph?" Winnie asks.

I put down my fork. How did she know?

Mom's off with Baby Maggie, Dad has already left for work, and Sandra is somewhere else in the house. Probably her room. Probably texting her boyfriend, Bo, who probably never gets stomachaches, because he's a baseball player and always smiles and does fun things like have doughnut-eating contests with Sandra.

But that means Winnie and I are alone. No one is listening in.

"When I was in fifth grade, a girl in my class broke her arm," Winnie says.

"Why?" I ask.

"She didn't mean to. But it happened during recess, with everyone there to see, and she cried and got rushed off to the hospital. It was very dramatic."

I imagine an arm with a bone sticking out of it. I'd cry, if I had that arm.

"And then the next day she came to school with a cast," Winnie goes on, "and guess what?"

"She broke her other arm?"

She laughs. "No. But everyone thought she was so cool, like a rock star."

That sounds about right, because the same thing would happen in Mrs. Webber's class if something very dramatic happened. Like when

Lexie got hit in the head with Mrs. Webber's clog last week, or like yesterday, when Joseph came back and everyone hogged him because *he* was the rock star.

I don't care if he's a rock star. I just don't want everyone hogging him.

Thinking about it makes me not feel so good, and I drop my gaze.

"Hey," Winnie says. "Ty." She lifts my chin. "It's normal, whatever you're feeling."

"What *am* I feeling?" I ask, because that's part of the problem. I honestly don't know, not for certain.

"Lots of things, probably," Winnie says. Her brown eyes lock with mine, and there is not a speck of meanness in them. Not a speck of *you're wrong* or *I'm disappointed in you* or *it's your own fault for not expecting the unexpected.*

"But there's more to my story," she says. "Maxine came back with a cast, like I said, and she got all kinds of crazy attention."

"Like a rock star?"

"Yeah, so guess what I did?"

"Maxine was the girl who broke her arm?"

"Uh-huh. I went outside after I got home from school and climbed the climbing tree, the one in the backyard." She makes a funny expression. "I went all the way out on the branch, as far as I could, and I dangled and dangled, trying to work up the courage to fall. Except Mom saw what I was doing and said, 'If you break your arm on purpose, I am *not* taking you to the emergency room.'"

"But she would have if you really did," I say.

"Eh," Winnie says. "Probably."

I tilt my orange juice glass, but not enough to spill any. With Winnie and Maxine . . . I *think* I get it. Winnie thought if she traded places with Maxine, or if her arm traded places with Maxine's arm, then everyone would have crowded around her instead of Maxine.

But with me and Joseph, it's different.

Winnie wanted the "everyone" part. I just want Joseph. I'm not sure how I feel about the "every-one else" part.

Winnie stabs a bite of my eggs with her fork and puts it in her mouth. "But after a few days, things went back to normal. Okay?"

I nod. I'm still confused, but I definitely like the idea of things going back to normal.

As soon as I get to school, I can see that it hasn't happened yet. Things *haven't* gone back to normal.

Part of it might be Joseph's red hat. Red is a hard color to look away from, for one thing, and the second thing is that nobody else is wearing a hat. Nobody at all. So his hat is like a cast, sort of, and everyone swarms all over him again.

Finally Mrs. Webber gets tired of it. She turns around from the whiteboard and puts down the marker.

"You kids are driving me crazy!" she says about all the whispering and fidgeting and fake pencil sharpening going on. Kids want an excuse to pass Joseph's desk. That's why they keep sharpening their pencils.

Joseph looks worried. So does Elizabeth, who is squatting beside him. She got out of her seat a few minutes ago in order to tell Silas to go back to *his* seat, but she stayed on after Silas left.

"These rascals can't leave you alone for a moment, can they?" Mrs. Webber says to Joseph. Elizabeth tries to sneakily duckwalk back to her desk, but ducks are probably the least sneaky animals in the world other than hippopotamuses.

"Elizabeth, I can see you, you know," Mrs. Webber says, and Elizabeth topples over. Her legs splay in front of her and her hair falls out of her barrette. Everyone laughs but me.

"Joseph, would you like to come up front and let everyone ask all the questions they're so desperate to ask?" Mrs. Webber says. "And then maybe, just maybe, we can focus on fractions?"

Everyone says please and makes begging hands, and Joseph rises from his desk and walks to the front of the room. That's where we stand when we do recitations, except Joseph hasn't done a recitation for ages.

"All right. If you'd like to ask Joseph a question, raise your hand," Mrs. Webber says.

Lexie's hand shoots into the air. She doesn't say "ooo ooo, pick me, pick me," because she knows Mrs. Webber doesn't like that, but she *does* perch on her bottom and make herself as tall as she can.

"Yes, Lexie?" Mrs. Webber says.

"I have a comment, not a question," Lexie says. "It's about my bruise. Do you remember my bruise? From last week, when you kicked me in the head?"

Mrs. Webber sighs. "I did not kick you in the head, Lexie, and we're not here to talk about your bruise. Those days are over."

"No, because it hasn't gone away yet," Lexie says. "See?"

She pushes her hair off her forehead, and her bruise is a good one, I admit. It's bluish purple in the middle, but turning yellow around the edges.

"Ooo-eee! Makin' bacon!" Taylor says.

"Absolutely not, Taylor," Mrs. Webber says sternly. "Now. Who has a real question?"

Taylor sticks up his hand. Mrs. Webber gives him a look, and he slumps and puts it down.

Claire raises her hand. Claire is a good kid and not too rascally, so Mrs. Webber says, "Joseph, would you like to call on Claire?"

"Um, Claire?" Joseph says.

"Are you better now?" she asks.

"Well, my doctor says I'm cured," Joseph says. "So . . . yeah."

"Did it hurt?" Elizabeth says.

"Did what hurt?" Joseph says.

"Being in the hospital."

"Oh. Um, I guess."

Chase raises his hand.

"Chase?" Joseph says.

"My sister went to the hospital when she had appendicitis, and she had one of those pole things that gives you fluids," Chase says.

"An IV?" Joseph says.

"Yeah, that. It made her have to go to the bathroom *all* the time."

Everyone laughs. Joseph does, too, but he twists his hands at the same time.

He calls on Lexie, even though she's already had a turn to talk. She says, "Did you know that a bruise means having dead blood trapped under your skin? That's why bruises turn different colors. It's the blood dying more and more until it goes away."

"Oh," Joseph says.

"I'm not sure that's entirely accurate, Lexie," Mrs. Webber says.

"It is," Lexie says. "Red, blue, purple, green, yellow, and brown. I'm almost to the brown stage."

Mrs. Webber says we should get back on topic. She calls on Natalia.

"Not to be rude," Natalia says, "but are you bald?"

Joseph blushes. "No. But . . . sort of."

Excitement ripples around the room. I raise my hand.

"Ty," Joseph says.

"I think being bald is cool," I say. "All the way bald *or* partway bald."

He's glad I said that. I can see it on his face.

"In fact, I'll probably shave my head when I grow up," I continue. "I'll have a shiny bald head, and it'll be awesome."

"Me too!" Taylor says. "*And* I'll be a race-car driver."

Beside me, John tugs on his hair. I can tell he's thinking that he might want to be bald, too. Lexie tells everyone that if she was bald, we could see her bruise better, and Taylor says, "Shut up about your bruise already!"

"Hey!" Lexie says.

"Taylor, we don't say 'shut up' in this classroom," Mrs. Webber says. "You know that." She picks up the egg timer she uses for time-outs, and Taylor says, "Aw, man." Then he calls Lexie a weenis. I don't know what a weenis is, but it's a word that makes everyone giggle and talk out of turn.

Mrs. Webber closes her eyes.

Elizabeth raises her hand and doesn't wait to be called on. She cries, "Mrs. Webber, Mrs. Webber, Lester escaped again!"

"What?!" Mrs. Webber says. Her eyes fly open. "No. Please tell me he didn't."

"He's not in his aquarium," Elizabeth says, pointing. "He's gone!"

There is a madhouse of girls squealing and drawing their legs off the floor and onto their chairs. John squeals and pulls his legs up, too.

His knees bang the bottom of his desk, and a container of pens and pencils goes flying.

Chase and Taylor and Lexie get out of their seats to look for Lester. So do other kids.

I go to Joseph and say, "Let's look behind the bookshelves. He likes dark places."

We go, and we look, but Lester isn't back there.

Joseph sets off to search somewhere else, but I grab his wrist.

"Um . . . we should keep a lookout," I say. "Just in case."

Joseph pulls his eyebrows together. Then he lets them relax. He slides his back along the wall and sits down.

"Taylor is loud," he says.

"I know," I say, sliding down next to him.

"Even louder than he used to be."

"I know."

There is chaos all around us, but Joseph and I have the book nook to ourselves. We watch people shriek and run around.

"Does Lester escape a lot?" Joseph asks.

"Not a *lot* a lot. Maybe once a week." I straighten my legs. "Mrs. Webber keeps trying to give him away, but nobody will take him."

"*I* would, except there's no way my mom would say yes," Joseph says.

"Same with mine," I say. "And it's too bad, because Teensy Baby Maggie needs a pet, but oh well."

"Huh?" Joseph says.

"Teensy Baby Maggie," I explain. "She needs a pet."

"She does? Why?"

For a second I can't come up with an answer. Why *does* Maggie need a pet?

I almost say, "Because I said so," but that's the kind of thing a kindergartner might say, or even a preschooler.

"She just does," I say.

"What would she do with it?"

"Be nice to it. Feed it crackers. I don't know."

"Feed it crackers?"

"That part's not important. The important part is that my mom said no to five thousand of my good ideas, but guess what? She said yes to a bird!"

Joseph tilts his head. "Why a bird?"

"Why not a bird?"

"A parrot?"

I'm getting frustrated, and my fingers tighten into a fist. "Not a parrot, because parrots don't live in the wild. My mom's one rule is that I have to catch the bird myself."

"Huh? *How?!*"

"Agh! I don't know! Maybe with a butterfly net! But if I do catch a bird—" I open my fingers and press them hard on the floor. "I mean, *when* I catch a bird, I get to keep it."

"Cool," Joseph says. He hesitates. "But . . . I thought you were giving it to Baby Maggie."

"We'll share. Also, Lexie thinks I can't, so I *have* to catch one to prove her wrong."

Joseph doesn't get it, I can tell. Then I remember that he doesn't know about our recitations last week. Mrs. Webber made us do an act of kindness, and I wanted my kindness to be a pet for Maggie, only it didn't work out. The bird-catching bit was part of my speech to the class, but Joseph didn't hear my speech.

I press the back of my head against the wall.

Joseph really was gone a long time.

He missed *a lot.*

I don't mind helping him catch up, and I don't mind all his questions. Not truly. I *do* mind everyone else in the world hogging his attention . . . but that isn't happening this very second, so why do I feel like there's a hole in my chest?

I feel this same way at bedtime every so often, after Mom and Dad kiss me and say good night and then go away. It's a feeling of being lonely, and it comes to me with a shock that I miss Joseph.

I miss him even though here he is beside me. I DON'T *KNOW* WHY.

I look at Joseph. Joseph looks at me.

"Found him!" Chase proclaims, holding Lester in the air.

And *yay* for Lester, I guess, but I still feel lost.

CHAPTER FOUR

On Wednesday, I come up with an idea. Actually, two ideas.

First, I go to my closet and pull out my secret candy bag, which is filled with candy from birthday parties and Halloween and Valentine's Day. It's basically filled with any candy that comes my way, and I don't even have to eat it to get the "feel better" feeling it gives me.

I like to feel how heavy it is and gaze inside at the different colored wrappers. I like to dribble fun-size Snickers and Dum Dums and Jolly Ranchers through my fingers. It's like I'm a pirate and the candy is my gold.

This morning, I dig around in my candy bag until I find my special cinnamon lollipop. The lollipop part is round, like a Ping-Pong ball, only it's red instead of white. Its wrapper says, "WARN-ING! CONTAINS FIERY CINNAMON FLAMES!", which is how I know what flavor it is.

I go downstairs and put the lollipop in my backpack.

Now for the second part of my idea. I root through the junk drawer until I find the long stretchy Ace bandage I like to use when I'm wounded. I find Winnie, give her the bandage, and stick out my arm.

"Will you?" I ask.

"Oh my gosh," she says. "Please tell me you're not pretending to be Maxine."

"I'm not!"

"And yet you want me to wrap your arm up like you've got a cast."

Yes. Well. But I'm not pretending to be *Maxine.* I'm just being someone—me—with a broken arm.

Winnie snorts and takes the bandage. "Fore-
arm, elbow, or both?"

"Both."

Sandra glances over from the sink. She's load-
ing the dishwasher since Mom is upstairs with
Baby Maggie. "Why are you pretending to have a
broken arm?"

"Because of Joseph," Winnie says, answering
for me.

My face gets hot. "No."

"Yeah-huh, because he's getting all the attention and you want some, too."

"No! I *hate* attention!"

Winnie and Sandra look at each other. They
laugh.

"Sure, tiger," Sandra says. "Whatever you say."

I clamp my lips together. What I'm going to
say is nothing, because I'm mad at them, because
they've gotten me all confused again.

When I had the idea of bandaging my arm,

I didn't think, *Ha-ha, and now I will steal all of Joseph's attention!*

I thought, *Ooo! If I show up with a broken arm, then at least half the class will switch from Joseph and his red hat to me and my cast. Half will bother him, and half will bother me, which means the bothering will be split between us. Which means more of Joseph will be up for grabs. Yeah!*

"Hey, it's your arm," Winnie says. "You can do whatever you want."

I know I can, but she doesn't understand. It's not me doing whatever I want. It's me trying to even things out. I guess I won't *mind* if everyone crowds around me and says, "Oh no! Ty! Your poor arm!" I won't yell at them or anything.

But I'm almost totally positive that the *real* reason for my cast is to get more Joseph-time for me, and more Ty-time for Joseph. More Joseph-and-Ty-time, period.

Winnie circles the bandage up and over my

arm. She tugs the end tight and tucks it under the top layer. "There. Beautiful."

Sandra comes over. She nods her approval and says, "We should sign it."

"Ooo, yeah," Winnie says.

Sandra grabs some Sharpies, plonks them on the kitchen table, and calls me over. Winnie joins us. I'm still a little bit mad at Winnie for not knowing the truth of what's inside me, but I sit down with them at the table.

"L-o-l-a" Sandra writes on the bandage, using fancy, loopy cursive.

"Who's Lola?" I say.

"It's to give you an air of mystery," Sandra says. "'Who *is* this Lola?' your friends will ask. 'Is she French?'"

Winnie puts her hand to her chest. "And you'll gaze off into the distance like this"—she makes her expression dreamy—"and say, 'Ah, *oui*. Lola, *mon petit chou*! How I miss her!'"

"What's a *p'tee shoe*?" I ask.

"A cabbage," Winnie says. "And now, some normal names." She picks a red Sharpie and writes "BOB" in blocky capital letters. With a green Sharpie, she writes "Al."

"*Al?*" Sandra says. "Who names their kid *Al*?"

"Who names their kid *Lola*?" Winnie says. Switching to a blue Sharpie, she writes "Serena." She twists my arm over, and Pamela, Melyssa, and Jenny all sign my cast. Jenny adds "Feel better!" and throws in a smiley face.

I admire my cast. It looks awesome.

"Now listen, Ty," Winnie says. "Nobody's going to believe you actually broke your arm." She holds up her finger. "But! They *might* believe you sprained your wrist or something."

"What's your cover story?" Sandra asks.

I tap my chin. The last time I wore my bandage, it was because I was a spy who'd gotten bitten by a poisonous earwig right on the ankle. Earwigs like arms just as much as ankles, I bet.

"A *believable* cover story," Winnie says.

"But—"

"*Ty . . .*" she says.

So no earwigs. Fine.

Oh! But yesterday after school, I did some bird-catching in the backyard. It was because of Chase and how he captured Lester and thrust him into the air, crying, "Found him!"

I imagined doing the same thing, only with a bird instead of a snake, and without the thrust-ing part, since squeezing a bird tightly isn't a good idea. I made up a whole movie in my head of how it would go.

First, I would cup the bird gently and hand it to Joseph.

"Here," I'd say.

"Wow," he'd say. He'd look at the bird, and then he'd lift his head and look at me. His expression would be happy and there wouldn't be any weirdness between us at all. "Wow, Ty. Thanks!"

When I think about it now, my movie doesn't make much sense.

But that doesn't mean I'm giving up on catching a bird.

Yesterday, I did all kinds of creeping and leaping and being-sneaky-ing, but all I ended up with was a scratch on my arm.

Scratches *are* real, though. Realer than earwigs.

I tell Sandra and Winnie that my scratch is my cover story.

Sandra says, "Hmm."

Winnie says, "Yeah, because I didn't see any scratches when I wrapped you up."

"There is one," I assure her. "I snuck up on this one very cute bird, and I did a flying tackle, and I landed on a stick."

"Birds are hard to catch," Winnie admits.

"Sticks, on the other hand . . ." Sandra says.

"At school, make it more than a scratch," Winnie says. She purses her lips. "Tell them you bruised your bone."

"Can you do that?" I say. "Bruise your bone?"

"Sure," Winnie says. "Happens all the time."

Mom comes downstairs carrying Baby Maggie. "Girls? Ty?" she says. "Shouldn't you be heading to school?" She notices my bandage. "Oh, honey, what happened?"

Sandra, Winnie, and I answer at the same time:

"Gangrene," Sandra says.

"Just a flesh wound," Winnie says.

"I bruised my bone," I say.

Mom takes it all in. "Ah. So the bandage is just for fun."

"*No,*" I say. "You don't need to take me to the hospital, but my bandage is *not* for fun."

Changing the subject seems like a better idea than trying to explain yet again, so I hop up, grab my backpack, and say, "Hey, what's a weenis?"

Mom, Sandra, and Winnie swivel their heads toward me. Maggie grabs a handful of Mom's hair.

Dad jogs down the stairs wearing his man shoes. He glances from face to face. "What'd I miss?"

"I asked what a weenis is," I say.

"The tip of your elbow," he answers.

Mom and the girls swivel their heads toward him.

"For real?" I say.

"For real," he says.

Winnie scrunches her nose. "Weenis means the tip of your elbow?"

"Joel, how on earth do you know that?" Mom says.

"Sweetheart, I know everything," he says. He winks at me. I grin.

Sandra puts down her phone, which she's been tapping on. "Holy moly, it does. I just looked it up."

So now I'm armed with my giant lollipop, my broken arm, and my weenises. Two of them, since I have two elbows.

I'm prepared for anything.

CHAPTER FIVE

I want to give Joseph the giant lollipop right away, but when I get to school, Mrs. Webber has already started morning meeting and I have to scurry to sit down with the others. The kids sit on the floor and Mrs. Webber sits in the chair from her desk, which she rolls to the center of the room. These days, she asks someone to crawl forward and lock the wheels, because last week her chair rolled out from under her. She fell backward, and her wooden clog flew off her foot and hit Lexie smack in the head. That's how Lexie got her bruise.

Mrs. Webber launches into her "Here's what we're going to do today" speech, and I scooch toward Joseph.

"Look," I whisper, holding out the arm with the cast on it.

His eyes widen. He reaches out to touch the bandage, then changes his mind and draws back his hand. "Are you okay?"

"I bruised my bone."

"Your *bone*?"

I catch Mrs. Webber glancing at us, so I sit up taller and put on my Good Listener face. "I'll tell you later," I say out of the side of my mouth. "Be sure to sit with me at lunch."

He gives me a thumbs-up.

After morning meeting, we do math. Then comes reading time. I sit at my desk and read *Sink or Swim*, which is about a brother and sister who fall into fairy tales and do funny things. Joseph is at his desk reading *Darth Paper Strikes Back*. Taylor is at the computer and taking one of the tests that says either yes, you really did read a certain book, or no, you didn't and you only said that you did.

"I passed!" he says when his score flashes up on the screen. He sounds amazed. "Mrs. Webber, Mrs. Webber, I passed!"

"Taylor, that's wonderful," Mrs. Webber says. She gives him a smile, because reading isn't easy for him. She says, "Class?"

"Hooray, hooray, hooray!" everyone cries. That's what we do when anyone passes a reading test.

Taylor beams. I'm glad for him. Then something hits my cheek, and my fingers go to my face. *Ow.* What was the thing, and where did it come from?

I hear a whistle. It's Lexie, who jerks her head to say, *By your feet, dumb-dumb.*

I reach down and scoop up a small paper airplane. It's a good one, with sharp creases, equal-sized wings, and a pointy nose that's pointy even after crashing into me.

I'm impressed, because I am not the best at

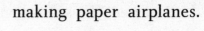 making paper airplanes. Instead of zooming through the air, my paper airplanes do nosedives or sad, floppy loop de loops. I'm good at other things, though. I can fling a playing card so fast that it slices through a Kleenex. Also, I can make George Washington's head turn into a mushroom by folding a dollar bill a special way. And I know *how* to make paper airplanes. They just never turn out right.

Lexie whistles again. She pretends to open a book, which is her silent way of saying, *Unfold the note, stupid-head.*

Oh. Okay. I unfold the paper airplane. It says, *What happened to your arm? xxx, Elmoneyfreshdogg.*

Right away a second paper airplane zings me. This one says, *Is that your fake bandage? We're not allowed to bring toys to school, you know. xxx, Moo Moo.*

My ribs tighten and I don't look her way. I forgot that she and I played with my Ace bandage one time when she came home with me after school. I wrapped her ankle up. Then she wrapped my ankle up. Then I wrapped her face up like a mummy, only with room for her to breathe. Then she wrapped me up like a mummy, only without room to breathe.

But bruised bones are real. They happen all the time. And Ace bandages aren't toys.

"Aren't you going to answer?" Lexie whispers.

I read my book. Or, I stare at the pages anyway.

Since it's a warm day, Mrs. Webber says we can eat lunch outside. I hurry to my backpack and dig out the giant lollipop, which I stick in my front pocket. It makes a lump. Then I grab my sack lunch. I'm careful

to use my good arm and not my hurt arm, in case anyone's watching. But I'm no longer sure the bandage was a good idea.

"Is your arm okay?" Joseph asks after we claim a picnic table. "Does it hurt?"

I wave off his question and pull out a peanut butter and jelly sandwich.

He pulls out a Go-GURT.

"I'm fine," I tell him. "I have a small flesh wound, but no one's worried about gangrene."

His eyebrows fly up. "Gangrene?"

Oops. Shouldn't have mentioned gangrene, not if the point is to be fine and *not* talk about my arm. I take a bite of my sandwich—a big bite—and use my chewing time to try and find something else to talk about.

Oh! Winnie told me a joke a few days ago, and I still remember it. I swallow and say, "Hey, Joseph, did you know that in Africa, a minute passes *every sixty seconds*?"

"Really?" Joseph says. "Cool."

Then he frowns.

I wait, fighting back my smile.

A grin splits his face. "Ha-ha. I get it."

"A minute passes every sixty seconds," I say, pleased. "Because a minute *is* sixty seconds."

"Yeah, I get it," he repeats. He squeezes out a bite of Go-GURT. "But for real. What happened to your arm?"

"Well . . . um . . ."

"Did you fall?"

"Kind of," I say, and then some part of me makes me decide to just tell the truth. And the second I decide that, I feel better. Lighter. Plus, it *is* my arm, after all. I can do what I want, just like Winnie said.

I put down my sandwich and lean in. "I'm going to tell you something, but I need you to promise—*promise*—not to tell anyone else."

"Okay."

"Yesterday, I was out catching a bird for Baby Maggie—"

"Did you catch one?"

"No, but I almost did. But anyway, I might have scratched my arm, and might *might* mean yes, and that *might* be the reason, you know, for . . ."

"For your bandage," Joseph says. He doesn't seem mad. He just seems interested. "Is it a bad scratch?"

"Well . . . not exactly," I say.

"Did it bleed?"

I giggle. "Um . . . not exactly?"

He giggles with me. "Did it even break the skin?"

"Um . . . not exactly?"

"What about your bone? Is your bone at least bruised?"

"*Well* . . ." I say, stretching it out to be silly, and then we finish together:

"Not exactly!"

A *bum bum bum* noise reaches my ears. It's the sound of feet marching our way. Too many feet. The feet in the front belong to Lexie, and my stomach clenches.

I talk to Joseph fast and low. "But don't tell. You promised, remember? And especially don't tell Lexie."

Joseph glances at the marchers. They're getting closer. "Then we need to talk about something else. We need to be talking when they get here."

"Right. Yes. Um, nose hair?"

"Earwax?"

"No—shoehorns! My dad has a shoehorn, and when you blow it, it goes, '*Shoooooooe!*'"

"What goes '*shoooo*'?" Lexie says.

"A shoehorn?" I say.

Joseph and I laugh. Lexie narrows her eyes. Elizabeth is with her, and Hannah and John and Chase and Silas and Taylor. They all squeeze into our table, which is only meant for four people.

Actually, it's only meant for me and Joseph.

"Don't believe him, people," Lexie says. "A shoehorn does not go '*shoo.*'"

"What *is* a shoehorn?" Elizabeth whispers to Hannah.

Lexie puts her hand up to tell them to hush.

"We want to know how you got hurt," she says, jabbing my bandaged arm.

"He bruised his bone," Joseph says.

Lexie rolls her eyes. "*Riiiight.* And who are all these people who signed their names?"

"Well . . . they're Chloe and Bob and Serena," I say.

"Al?" Lexie says. She turns over my arm. "*Lola?*"

"Lexie, you're being too rough," Joseph says. "You need to be gentle."

"Or what? I'll bruise his bone more? Unwrap your arm and show us, because I know bruises, believe me."

My body gets hot on the inside and prickly cold on the outside.

"You can't see a bruised bone," Joseph says. "Right, Ty?"

He's trying hard. But Lexie will try harder. I know she will, and she'll never give up, and now lunch is ruined. Joseph didn't ruin it. Lexie did. Or maybe I did by wearing this stupid bandage in the first place.

I leave. I get up and walk away from the picnic table altogether.

"Ty, why are you leaving?" Joseph asks.

"Don't go after him," Lexie says.

"But—"

"Joseph, sit," Lexie commands. "If Ty wants alone time, let him have alone time."

Taylor says something about his boogers, and Elizabeth says, "Nasty."

"But where are you going, Ty?" Joseph calls.

I don't answer, and pretty soon his voice blends with all the others.

I go to my private spot under the play struc-
ture. I scoot on my bottom until I'm all the way in,
and then I lean against a metal pole that's part of
the bouncy bridge.

I unwrap the bandage from my arm. I dig
through the dry sand on top until I get to the
damper sand underneath. I always get to damp
sand eventually, and when I do, that's when I
know I've gone deep enough.

I scoop and scoop until I've got the right size
hole. I roll up the bandage and shove it in. I pile
the wet sand on top of it, and then I fill in the
rest with dry sand. I push my hair out of my eyes
and examine my work. *Hmm.* It looks pretty good,
but I sprinkle some small rocks around for good
measure.

I rest my head on my arms. I'll stay here until
Mrs. Webber calls us in, I decide. If Lexie wants
me to have alone time so much, then I will.

"You have sand in your hair," someone says.

My head flies up.

"Your hands and knees are sandy, too," the someone says. It's Breezie. She's sitting farther back in a shady spot. There are shadows all over her.

"I know," I say. "It's a playground." My heart is racing. "What are you doing here?"

"What are *you* doing here?"

We stare at each other. Neither one of us wants to bring up Lexie. Neither of us wants to bring up Joseph.

Breezie looks away first, but she pretends she didn't lose the staring contest by gesturing at my front pocket.

"What's that lump?"

I pull out the giant red lollipop. It feels like a month since I got it out of my candy bag. A year.

"Can I have it?" Breezie asks.

Well. I don't know the rule about this. I brought the lollipop for Joseph, but Joseph isn't here.

Breezie is.

And she's a girl.

And her hair is pretty and long.

"I won't tell," she says. I know she's talking about the Ace bandage, not the lollipop.

I make my arm as straight as a stick and hold out the lollipop.

"I was going to give it to you anyway," I say.

Her eyes are sad, but she halfway smiles. "Thanks."

CHAPTER SIX

When we're back inside from lunch, Lexie takes one look at me and says, "Where'd your bandage go?"

"*Mmm-MMM-mmm,*" I say, shrugging.

I side-eyeball Breezie. She's pretending to organize her desk, but her face says *la-la-la, this time I'm choosing with Ty.*

Lexie doesn't let up about it, and Taylor and Chase say things too, like, "Yeah, Ty, do you have magical healing powers? Is that how your arm got better so fast?"

Breezie doesn't join in, and neither does Joseph. I'm glad about that, but I feel guilty for abandoning him at lunch. Also, I'm embarrassed about "alone time." So even though I know that

Joseph is on my side, it doesn't feel like we're a team.

I don't wear the bandage the next day, since *duh*, I buried it. But I wouldn't have anyway. My bandage days are over. Lexie bugs me about it *anyway*, copying Chase by asking if I have healing powers and if I'm a wizard and if I can turn people into frogs, stuff like that. To the frog question, I say, "Yep, people like you," and keep doodling in my notebook.

So *ha*.

Joseph and I sit together at lunch, but it's not just us. There are other kids, too. I help Joseph with his fractions worksheet, because he wasn't here when we started fractions. Everything's fine, I guess. But I don't know. We both might be pretending we're back to being best friends more than we really are.

Breezie's opinion is that Joseph is everybody's

new best friend. That's what she says to me by the water fountain. "He thinks he's so important," she adds, picking an invisible piece of dust off her dress.

"I don't think he thinks that," I say.

"Well, I do. It's annoying."

I guess she's missing Lexie. I guess she wants Lexie to leave Joseph and come back to her.

I guess I wish that, too.

I imagine the universe the way I drew it on Monday, with the planets all in the wrong places and space junk floating randomly. I'm beginning to wonder if the universe is ever going to line up straight again.

After school, Mom picks me up and tells me we have one errand to run.

"Blah," I say, feeling sorry for myself. I just want to go home and watch cartoons, but I don't get to, so I roll the car window up and down. I lock and unlock my door. I do both of these over and over.

"Ty? Stop," Mom says.

I slump. Next to me, Baby Maggie wiggles in her car seat, kicking her chubby feet to make her socks come off. It's cute, because she doesn't even need socks. She's a baby. But how come she's allowed to be squirmy and I'm not?

Mom glances at me in the rearview mirror. She says, "What's going on, bud?"

I press my lips together. How do my mom and my sisters always know when to ask that question?

"Well, it's just . . . Joseph," I say. "He thinks he's so important, just because he's finally back from the hospital."

"*Ty,*" Mom says. I know she's disappointed in me. I'm disappointed in me, too.

"It was Breezie who said that," I say in a small voice. "I know it's not true. I even told Breezie it's not."

"Hmm," Mom says.

"For real. Mom, that really is the truth."

Mom exhales. "Oh, baby. It's hard, isn't it?"

I blink. I was waiting for a scolding. Cautiously, I say, "What's hard?"

"Life," she says. She reaches back and squeezes my knee. "But you'll get through it, and that is also the truth. For real."

She pulls into the parking lot of Collindale Care Center, and my heart sinks. Collindale Care Center is a nursing home. Every month, Mom visits an old lady named Eloise who lives here. I guess today is Eloise Day. I guess that's the errand.

Mom parks the car and turns to face me. "I know that visiting Eloise isn't your favorite thing to do," she says, and I pick invisible dust off me like Breezie did at the water fountain. "But doing something nice for someone might make you feel better, if you let it. You might be surprised."

I don't think so, because when we go inside, it smells the way it always does. The paint on the walls is the same yucky yellow, and the lightbulbs they use make my eyes hurt. Also, I know Eloise won't let me make her bed go up and down, so I don't even ask.

Joseph, when I used to visit him at the hospital, let me make his bed go up and down as much as I wanted.

Eloise makes "ooh-ooh" noises when she sees Teensy Baby Maggie. She reaches out a shaky hand, and Mom steps closer with Maggie in her arms. Eloise pats Maggie's leg. She and Mom start talking about baby stuff, and I push down a groan.

I leave Eloise's room and wander into the hall. I'm allowed, and Mom sees me go out the door and nods to say it's okay, so it's not like I'm secretly escaping or anything.

But—aha! Outside in the hall, in his motorized wheelchair, is Mr. Marconi, who is scary and strange and interesting. Mr. Marconi doesn't like it at the Collindale Care Center, and he's *always* trying to secretly escape. Really!

I press my back against the wall. I don't want Mr. Marconi to see me, because he has the bushiest eyebrows in the world. Eyebrows that could kill a small animal, Winnie says.

I don't know *how* his eyebrows would do that, but I believe her. If I were a small animal and I saw those eyebrows coming, I would run like the wind.

"Hey, kid," Mr. Marconi says.

I pretend not to hear him.

"Hey!" he says. "Kid!"

I point at my chest. "Me?"

He gestures for me to come over. His chin sinks into his chest, making him look like a human version of quicksand. First his chin will sink all the way in, then his face, then his bushy eyebrows.

"Come on, come on," he says. "Speed it up before one of those old biddies comes and makes me play bingo."

I walk toward him, dragging my feet. He uses the joystick on his wheelchair to meet me halfway.

"What's your name, kid?" he says. He asks me this every time he sees me.

"Ty," I tell him.

"What kind of name is that?" he grouches. "Your mother named you after a tie? What's she going to do, tie you around your father's neck?"

He says this every time, too.

"It's short for Tyler," I say.

He waves his hand to say, *yeah yeah, not interested.* I can see the bones in his fingers, especially his knuckles.

"Listen," he says. He thinks he's whispering, but he's not. "I need to get out of here. They put me in here by mistake, see?"

He checks for old biddies. Then he points at the emergency exit door at the far end of the hall. "Open that door for me, kid. The bar's too heavy for me to press. But just open that door, and I'll take it from there."

"I'm sorry, Mr. Marconi. I can't."

"Aw, you." He makes a raspberry sound, like when Dad blows on Baby Maggie's tummy. I bet he makes a thousand raspberry sounds a day, or at least a hundred, because he's always asking people to open the exit for him, and no one ever does. Everyone knows he's supposed to stay in the building. It's one of the nursing home rules.

"So . . . bye, Mr. Marconi," I say.

His bushy eyebrows push lower and his chin sinks deeper. "Bah," he says, making his wheelchair turn in the other direction. He rolls away.

I wonder if I should go check on Mom and Eloise, because Mr. Marconi reminded me about bingo, and if there's a bingo game going on, I want to know. Mr. Marconi might not like bingo, but for me, bingo is the one fun thing at the nursing home. I get to play for the people who can't play on their own, and I get to use a big fat bingo marker to make blue dots on B-11 or G-58 or whatever. When the prize cart comes around, I get to help whoever I'm with decide between a piece of costume jewelry or a banana.

As I'm walking back to Eloise's room, I see a lady come out of another room.

"Bye for now, Mom," the lady says. She sniffles and dabs a Kleenex to the corner of her eye. "But I'll be back tomorrow. By then, I bet the nurses will have you completely settled in."

Whoever's in the room must be new, that's my guess. And her daughter—because that's who the lady must be—is worried about her because it's her first day here.

I cross the hall, thinking I'll tell the lady about bingo and crafts and all the other stuff they do here. It's actually not *that* bad. I just don't want to live here myself.

But she hurries off before I reach her. And then—*uh-oh.*

Mr. Marconi. He spots her, and his wrinkled hand goes to his joystick. With a zoom and a fast stop, he plants himself in front of her.

"Hey, you," I hear him say. He beckons her closer and speaks to her in his raspy voice.

The lady tucks away her Kleenex and says, "Of course, of course." She walks in her high heels toward the emergency exit.

I chase after her. "Um . . . ma'am? Lady?" I don't know what to call her!

Anyway, it's too late. She pushes the "emergency only" bar, and there's a buzz, and the metal door that says "emergencies only" swings open! And this *is* an emergency, but only because the lady turned it into one! She didn't know, but still!

"Mr. Marconi, wait!" I cry. "You can't go out there!"

He hunches his shoulders and jams his joystick forward. I break into a run.

"Stop him! He's not allowed!" I call.

Mr. Marconi is five feet away from the door. The lady who opened it for him looks confused.

He's four feet away. A nurse pops into the hall and calls to Mr. Marconi in a panicked voice.

He's three feet away, and *there is traffic outside,* and *a real live road with sidewalks and yellow lines and cars.*

The lady draws her hand to her mouth.

He's two feet away. One foot away. *He's going out the door.*

The nurse's hands flutter in the air. "Mr. Marconi! Mr. Marconi!"

She reaches the exit, but the doorway is too
narrow to fit both a nurse and a man in a wheelchair.

The traffic-y road is *right there*, just outside the
door.

I high-jump over Mr. Marconi's wheelchair. It
takes the highest jump ever to get over the arm-
rest *and* his knees *and* his feet, and I stumble
when I land.

"Out of the way!" Mr. Marconi yells. "Out of
the way, out of the way!"

Owwee, I think. But I turn toward him and
brace myself. I do *not* get out of the way.

Bam! goes his wheelchair, ramming into my
shins.

He backs up and does it again. *Bam!* It HURTS,
and I know I'm going to have bruises.

Inside the building, people speak loudly and

do frantic things with their hands. I spot Mom, who says, "Ty?"

Mr. Marconi rams me again. *Ow!*

I grab the armrests of his wheelchair. "Mr. Marconi, *no.*"

We fight for the joystick. He has crazy-eyebrow power, but I'm stronger.

The wheelchair stops.

I win.

Straining, I push him back into the building. The nurses flood around us, and Mom, and the lady. Everyone fusses over Mr. Marconi, but they also say, "Thank you, little boy," and "Ty! What in the world?!" and "If you hadn't been here, just think what could have happened!"

I put my hands on my thighs and lean over, breathing hard. *I'm not a little boy* is the first thing I think, but it doesn't bother me too much because I know adults are bad at guessing ages.

The second thing I think is, *I did it. I saved*

Mr. Marconi. Maybe he didn't want to be saved, but I saved him anyway—and it did *feel good.*

The third thing I think is, *Joseph.*

Thinking about him makes me sad and happy. Sad because our best-friend-ness isn't back to normal, but happy because it can't be *all* the way gone, not if he's the first person I want to tell about my crazy afternoon.

And he is.

CHAPTER SEVEN

Mom calls Dad from the nursing home parking lot and tells him the whole story. She laughs as she tells it, and I hear Dad laughing on the other end. I'm not sure how I feel about this, because I didn't know it was a funny story.

But as I listen, I start to smile. I guess it was pretty funny, with Mr. Marconi scowling and motoring forward and the nurse flapping her arms around.

If Mr. Marconi had gotten hit by a car, it wouldn't be. But he didn't.

"Absolutely," Mom says after she's reached the end of the story. "I know. I agree!" She listens for a moment, then laughs again. "If you say so. Bye, baby. Love you, too."

Mom ends the call and twists to face me. Her

eyes are soft and shiny. The softness is because she loves me, and the shininess is because her very own son rescued an old man in a wheelchair from escaping from Collindale Care Center.

Her very. Own. Son.

"Your dad is very proud of you, and so am I," Mom says. "In fact, I think we should go out and celebrate."

"Yeah!" I say.

"Your dad's busy, but how about I take you to Chipotle for dinner? Sandra and Winnie can fend for themselves."

"Can I get a Coke even though it's after two o'clock? Can we invite Joseph?"

Mom laughs. "No to the Coke, but yes to Joseph." She taps some buttons on her phone and hands it to me. "Here—you do the asking. If he says yes, I can talk to his mom after."

Joseph does want to come with us, and we drive straight from the nursing home to pick him up. He sprints out of his house wearing his fuzzy red hat, and when he slides into the backseat, he grins. I grin back. I'm glad it's just the two of us. I mean, Mom and Baby Maggie are here, but they aren't kids. They aren't Lexie or Taylor or Chase or Hannah or any of those people.

"Hi!" he says.

"Hi!" I say, and since it's the first time Joseph has EVER MET MAGGIE, who's sitting between us because the middle seat is the safest place for her car seat, I make her say "hi" to him, too.

I pick up her bitsy hand and flap it at Joseph. "Hi!" I say in a baby voice.

Joseph waves. Baby Maggie kicks her cute little feet.

"She sure is pink," Joseph says.

I tilt my head. "I guess she is."

Maggie *pluhs* at him, which means that she poofs out her lips and goes *pluh* and spits out a tiny spit bubble.

"That means she likes you," I say. "Also, she has hair sprouts now, which she didn't even a week ago." I fluff up a tuft of Maggie's pale brown hair. "See?"

"Me too," Joseph says, and he pulls his hat partway off.

"Awesome," I say. His hair is super short, but unlike Maggie's hair, which so far grows only in patches, Joseph's short hair covers his whole head. He looks like an army guy.

After that, Maggie wiggles and Mom drives, and I tell Joseph the Mr. Marconi story.

"Where did Mr. Marconi want to go?" Joseph asks.

"I don't know. Back to his old house?"

"But he can't go back to his old house," Joseph says, but there's a bit of a question in his eyes.

"I guess not. I guess he's too old."

"He probably can't live on his own anymore," Mom says, keeping her eyes on the road. "That's usually why people move into nursing homes."

"Or they get moved in there by someone else," I say, remembering the lady in the hall who'd dabbed her eyes with a Kleenex.

Mom nods. "Things change. Life goes on. It's not always easy."

I shift. Joseph fiddles with his seat belt. Then he brings up LEGOs, because we both love LEGOs. From there we go to Origami Yoda and chocolate-covered potato chips, which I've never heard of.

"Really?" Joseph says. "You've really never heard of them?"

"I've really never heard of them."

Lexie, if she knew about something that no one else did, would be a show-off about it. Like, she'd brag about how good chocolate-covered potato chips were to make the rest of us feel like we were missing out.

But Joseph isn't Lexie. He sits up taller and says he'll bring me some tomorrow.

At Chipotle, Joseph and I both order chicken

quesadillas and chips, and Mom lets us get Izzes for our drinks, since they don't have caffeine. We both pick the orange kind, which is called Sparkling Clementine.

The guy at the cash register asks if Joseph and I each want a rubber bracelet. He has a big plastic container of them, and I wonder if the bracelets are like Chipotle's version of a kids' meal prize.

Joseph and I look at each other. "Sure," we say.

I take a blue one and slip it on. It says BUILDING A BETTER COMMUNITY.

Joseph picks a red one. It says CHANGING THE WORLD ONE DAY AT A TIME.

The guy behind the cash register says, "Looking good, dudes."

We eat on the patio. Mom and Baby Maggie sit at one table, and Joseph and I sit at another. The cheese in our quesadillas is warm and melty, and our Izzes are just the right amount of cold. I take a swig and let out a loud burp.

Joseph laughs. He takes a sip of his Izze and tries to burp, but no burp comes out. He tries again. Nothing.

"You have to swallow a sip of air," I say.

"I know, but I can't."

"Like this," I say, and I show him. I don't even drink any of my Izze, and still I make a nice, loud burp.

"*Ty,*" Mom says from the other table.

"Sorry!" I say. I giggle, expecting Joseph to giggle back. Instead, he stares at the iron picnic table.

I put down my drink. "Um . . . well . . . can you crack your knuckles?"

"No."

"Me neither. Plus, I'm not allowed."

"Taylor can," Joseph says. "Taylor cracks his knuckles all the time."

"Yeah, and it's annoying."

"And he can make himself burp. So can Chase

and John and every boy in our class. Even Lexie can make herself burp."

I don't know what to say.

"Does everyone think I'm weird?" he asks.

"Huh?"

"I can't burp. I can't crack my knuckles. I didn't even know about Lester," he says unhappily. "Why didn't you tell me about Lester?"

Lester, our class snake? Again, all I can say is *"Huh?!"*

He tugs his fuzzy red hat lower over his head. I have a just-out-of-reach feeling, like there's something I should be figuring out. Something I *could* be figuring out, if I could stretch up and pluck the answer from the sky.

Instead, a big black crow swoops down and plucks Joseph's quesadilla off the table. And then the crow takes off with it! Gone!

Another crow meets the first crow in the air. It snaps its beak and steals some for itself.

"Wow," I say.

Joseph's eyes are big. Together, we watch the crows.

"Check out all the crows by the trash can," he says.

"Whoa."

The metal trash can is overflowing with Chipotle wrappers and Dairy Queen cups and even some Dairy Queen unfinished ice-cream cones, and at least a dozen birds are fighting over the scraps of food. Maybe more.

Some are crows. Some are just regular birds. The regular birds are smaller than the crows, but they're quicker, and good at darting in for the fast grab.

"That one bird never gets any," he says, pointing at a small brown bird a couple feet from the trash can.

"Poor bird," I say.

The brown bird hops closer to the trash can,

but a bigger bird flies down and lands in front of him. The brown bird hops to the left. A crow caws and says, in bird language, "Get out of here, buddy." With its black flapping wings, the crow shoos the brown bird off.

"He can't fly," Joseph says. "That's why."

I study the bird. One of his wings flutters, but the other one doesn't. He's able to hop around, but he never leaves the ground.

"You're right," I say.

Then it soaks in.

That bird *can't fly.*

I glance at Mom, who's talking on her phone and using her foot to rock Maggie in her car seat. I slowly stand up.

"Hey, Joseph," I whisper.

He's already with me. He stands up slowly and silently, too.

We both put our fingers to our lips.

We are going to catch that bird.

CHAPTER EIGHT

One good thing about Lexie is that she taught me how to tiptoe while I'm wearing sneakers. The trick is to tiptoe *inside* my sneakers. Most people try to put their shoes down quietly, but the real way is to put your toes down quietly *inside your shoes,* and that makes your shoes go down quietly, too.

Joseph is also good at tiptoeing.

We approach the trash can from opposite directions. Animals know you're creeping up on them if you're obvious about it, so I gaze at the blue sky and think thoughts like, *Hello, blue sky. What a pretty color. And look! The sun's starting to set! Good job, sun.*

I think these thoughts loudly. My footsteps are quiet, and my thoughts are loud, and this way the birds can go about their business without having the bird-thought of, *Yikes! Big thing coming! FLY!*

We close in on the brown bird. We are so amazingly sneaky until a crow flaps its wings and caws, right in Joseph's face.

"Ahhhh!" Joseph cries.

The birds fly away in one big mass, and there goes our sneakiness. We burst out laughing, even though I'm sure we've scared every last bird away.

"Custard!" I say.

"Wait," Joseph says. "Look. Over there."

I scan the ground. The brown bird *isn't* gone.

He's just hiding behind the trash can. We move slowly toward him, and he hops as fast as he can. He *tries* to fly, but his wings don't work right.

Still, he's quicker than I am, because when I lunge for him, my hands close on empty air.

"Almost!" Joseph says.

"Try again," I say.

We circle the bird. He *definitely* can't fly, or he'd be gone already.

"We're not going to hurt you, bird," I tell him, since our cover has already been blown. I bet he's scared with the two of us looming over him. I don't want him to be.

"Boys?" Mom calls. She has one hand on Baby

Maggie's car seat and the other on her phone, which she's holding to her chest. "What are you two up to?"

Mothers are like birds. It's better, sometimes, if they don't know exactly what you're thinking.

"Just playing," I say, which is true. We're having fun, and that counts as playing. There's no need to say, "And the game we are playing is called Let's Catch a Bird."

"All right, well, I'm chatting with your aunt Lucy," Mom tells us.

Her remark might seem random, but it's not. Mom has her own Mom-language, just like the birds have bird-language and Joseph and I have boy-language.

I'm pretty good at Mom-language, though. What she's really saying is, *So please let me keep chatting, because I don't get the chance to talk to Aunt Lucy nearly enough. Life is so busy! And plus, Baby Maggie! So stay out of trouble and let me have a few minutes to myself. Will you do that for me, boys?*

I give her a thumbs-up. "Tell her 'hi' for me!"

Mom smiles. She puts her phone back to her ear and I hear her say, "Luce? I'm back. Now about this Sam guy . . ."

The birds that flew away are beginning to return. They pick at the leftovers in the trash can, but they make sure to keep an eye on me and Joseph.

"Sure is a nice night," I say casually. "Don't you think?"

"Huh?" Joseph says.

"And the sunset—isn't it beautiful?" From the side of my mouth, I say, "Play it cool. Don't let the crows make you go, 'Ahhhhh!' again."

"I didn't mean to the first time."

"Yeah, yeah, I'm just saying." I hook my thumbs through my belt loops and bounce lightly on the balls of my feet. *La la la, just out for a stroll.*

In my casual, talking-about-the-sunset tone,

I say, "You walk toward me, and I'll walk toward you. If we keep Fernando between us, then he can't get away."

"Fernando?"

"Don't. Laugh. Didn't we just cover this?"

"Fernando," Joseph states.

"Yes. Fernando. Now come on."

I step toward Fernando. His sugar eyes blink, and he hops toward Joseph. Joseph steps closer, and Fernando hops back toward me. He chirps, and Joseph and I look at each other. We grin.

Fernando hops back again and lands on my toe. *Eeek*! Fernando is on my toe! Joseph drops to his knees. His hands fly out and close around Fernando, and . . . omigosh! He has him! Joseph has Fernando!!!

"You did it!" I cry.

"I did!" Joseph says.

"You caught a bird, a real live bird! And Joseph, that is *way* cooler than burping!"

Joseph is so surprised by this news that his hands fall open and Fernando drops to the ground. He lands on the concrete with a *splumph*.

Joseph and I suck in our breath.

"*IS HE DEAD*?" Joseph asks in a too-loud whisper.

"*I DON'T KNOW*!" I loud-whisper back.

Joseph gulps. "Fernando?"

I squat and say, "Please be alive. Okay, Fernando? Please?"

Fernando twitches.

I hold perfectly still.

Fernando does a full-body quiver, and just like that he's back on his feet and hopping away in his extremely fast-hopping way.

"CATCH HIM!" Joseph and I yell.

It's a mad scramble. Joseph's elbow hits my eye, and my knee hits Joseph's shin. Then my knee lands on the asphalt—*ow*!—and it occurs to me in a far back part of my mind that I'll have another bruise, and possibly a nice bloody scrape.

Fernando hops and chirps—

And Joseph and I lunge and grab—

And this time *I* catch him. Fernando, not Joseph. His body is warm. His heart goes *drub-drub-drub-drub-drub* beneath my fingers.

My heart races, too, because . . . a bird! My very own bird! He flutters against my cupped hands, feathers and feet and a tiny sharp beak. It tickles. I'm suddenly afraid that *I* might drop him.

"Can I borrow your hat?" I ask Joseph.

"Why?"

"To put Fernando in, and also . . ." I glance at Mom, who's still on the phone. She's holding on to Baby Maggie's foot and laughing at whatever Aunt Lucy is saying. She's not paying attention to Joseph and me at all.

"Well, just in case," I say. "Only until I get Fernando home. Then I'll find someplace better."

"But you're dropping me off first."

"So?"

"So if Fernando is in my hat, I won't have it for tomorrow."

"So?"

Joseph looks away. He's either frustrated or embarrassed or both, and I'm pretty sure I know why. I want to tell him he doesn't need a hat, and that he can be bald or partway bald or not at all bald. Whatever he wants.

Instead, I say, "It's so soft and comfy-looking."

Joseph fingers the edge of his hat. I stay quiet.

He tugs it off and hands it to me. "Oh, fine."

I ease Fernando into Joseph's hat, and my heart swells. He's so tiny and cute in there.

"Thanks," I say.

Joseph rubs the back of his head. "You're welcome, but he *better* not poop in there."

CHAPTER NINE

Winnie thinks we should call Fernando "Sugar Daddy" instead of Fernando. I tell her that's not going to happen.

Mom says, for the fourth or tenth time that *keeping* Fernando isn't going to happen, either. She's so sorry, blah blah blah, but it just isn't feasible, sweetie.

I bow my head and don't listen. Plus, *feasible*. What's feasible? What I want is pleasable.

"Ty . . ." Mom says.

I can feel her looking at Dad, who is on her side because that's what they always do. They *always* have to be on each other's side.

We're in the den, having a family conference. I'm on the couch, and Fernando is in a shoebox

in my lap. Joseph's hat is in the shoebox, too, like a fuzzy red blanket. Fernando hasn't pooped *or* peed on it.

Winnie is sitting next to me. Sandra is sitting next to Winnie. Mom and Dad are standing by the fireplace, and Baby Maggie is in Dad's arms.

"Ty, bud, he's sick," Dad says.

"So? That means we should be nice to him, not say, 'Okay, and good-bye now.'"

"It's not that easy," Dad says.

"Why not?"

"Because he's a bird. An outdoor bird, and we don't know how to help him get better."

"We could call a bird doctor," I say.

"We could," Dad says carefully. "But I don't know any bird doctors."

"You could find one on the Internet. Or Mom could call Doctor Petty again," I say.

Dr. Petty's the vet who takes care of Sweetie-Pie. Her name really is Dr. Petty, with the "pet" part right in there, and Mom called her once already. It was right after we got home. We came in from the garage, and Mom plonked her purse on the island and shifted Baby Maggie from one arm to the other. Then she glanced at me and noticed Joseph's hat.

She said, "Ty, isn't that Joseph's hat? Why do you have Joseph's hat . . . and why are you holding it like that?"

So I told her, and I *showed* her, and she should have been a polite mommy and said, "Why, hello, Fernando. How nice to meet you."

Instead, she made a pained expression and

gave a speech that started with, "Oh, sweetie," and ended with me going *la la la* in my head because I didn't like what she was saying.

Then she dug her phone out of her purse and called Dr. Petty, only she reached a recording and not a real person. I heard Dr. Petty's faraway voice saying when the clinic was open and stuff like that, and then, at the end, "If this is an emergency, please call two-three-one-something-something-something."

And it *was* an emergency! It still is! But Mom didn't call that other number. She just pressed the hang-up button and set her phone by her purse with a sigh.

From her spot in the den, Mom sighs again. "This is my fault. I'm sorry, Ty. I never should have said yes to keeping a bird in the first place."

"But you did," I say.

"She didn't think you'd actually catch one," Dad replies.

A quivery feeling spreads over me. I'm so mad at him, and I'm so mad at Mom, too. Fernando is being a very small shape in the very corner of the box, and it doesn't make any sense but I'm mad at him, too. Couldn't he . . . perk up? Fluff his wing feathers and look around at everybody with his bright eyes?

Winnie runs her finger down Fernando's back.

"He's such a cutie," she says. She places her whole hand over his body, gently, and holds it there. Does she feel his heart beating? Does she feel him breathing? "He *is* sick, though."

"That's why you were able to catch him," Sandra adds. "Well, but you know that already."

Maybe I do, maybe I don't.

"What would you do if you did keep him?" Sandra goes on. "Keep him in that box? Do you think he would like that?"

"I'm not even sure he'd be that fun as a pet," Winnie says. She moves her hand from Fernando's body to my knee. "I'm not saying that to be mean."

I twitch my leg to get rid of her. She's being nice, because she's Winnie, but right now I'm trying not to cry, and niceness makes it worse.

"And what about Sweetie-Pie?" she says.

"What about Sweetie-Pie?"

"She's a cat. Cats like birds."

"Cats like to *eat* birds," Sandra says, in case I was too dumb to understand.

I hold the shoebox tighter. "We would keep him safe."

"None of us has ever taken care of an outside bird, or any bird," Mom says. "In your heart, I think you know that."

A stupid tear runs down my cheek. A lot of stupid tears. Winnie hugs me, and I bury my head against her side.

"I made a mistake, Ty," Mom says. "Grown-ups mess up, just like kids do."

"But you shouldn't," I say, my voice muffled by Winnie's shirt.

"But I did, and now my job is to figure out how to fix it. I hope you'll help."

I peek at her and see Dad pull her close. He kisses the top of her head.

I peek at Fernando. He's still in the corner of the box, just . . . sitting there.

I take a shuddery breath. I push myself up from Winnie and drag the back of my arm over my eyes.

"Okay, but we can't just put him back outside," I say. "How would *that* be helping him?"

"I agree," Winnie says.

"Me too," Sandra says. "I think you should call the emergency vet number, Mom."

Mom starts to protest. I bet she's going to say she doesn't want to bother Dr. Petty or something dumb like that. Then Mom's expression changes. She nods and says, "You're right. I can do that. I can, and so I will."

"Will you do it now?" I ask.

"Absolutely. I left my phone in the kitchen—I'll be right back." She slips out of the den, closing the door behind her.

"I'm sorry you're sad, Ty," Dad says. "Things don't always work out the way we want them to, do they?"

You think? I want to say, but I don't since that would be smart-mouthing. But I know more about things not working out then he ever will.

When Mom comes back, she tells us that Dr. Petty's assistant, Sam, is willing to come pick Fernando up, and Sam and Dr. Petty will do all they can to get Fernando well. Mom also tells me that even though birds from nature should be left in nature, Dr. Petty said I probably saved Fernando's life by bringing him home.

That's good, I guess. I hold Fernando's box in my lap until Sam arrives. Then I pet him one last time and say, "Get better." I don't want to be the

one to give him to Sam, so I hand the box to Winnie, who takes him to the front door.

After I see Sam's car pull away, I go to my room. I
lie on my bed. I think about birds and promises and
things not going how they're supposed to, and then
I call Joseph. I tell him everything that's happened.

"Oh," he says. He pauses. "Well, it's good that
we saved him."

"Yeah."

"And it's good that your vet can help him."

"Yeah."

We breathe.

"Baby Maggie still doesn't have a pet," I say.

"Maybe when she's older, you can get her
something," he says.

"I know," I say heavily. He's being kind about it,
even though he sat next to Baby Maggie in Mom's
car and saw that she really *is* a baby. Babies don't
need pets. Babies don't know what pets are. I pre-
tended Maggie wanted a pet, but it was me all along.

I swallow, needing to make some part of the day be worth it. "But catching him, that was fun."

Joseph tries to help out by laughing. "Remember when that crow flew into your face and you went, 'Ahhhh!'"

"That was you!" I say. "And then you jammed your elbow into my eye and practically made me blind?"

"You have two eyes. I only hit one, so you wouldn't have been *blind*."

"You never know about me."

"Um, yes I do."

"You know what, though?"

"What?"

I grip the phone, because this is the important thing. The thing I need to make sure Joseph understands. "The reason we had so much fun is because it was *us*. Just me and you."

"Well, your mom was there, and Baby Maggie."

"You know what I mean." I gather my courage. "At

school, I sometimes feel like you get stolen from me."

"Stolen?"

I speak quickly. "It's better when it's just us, that's all. So we should keep it that way, including at school. Deal?"

He's supposed to say, "Deal."

He's *not* supposed to go silent.

"Don't you want to be my best friend?" I say.

"Yes!"

"Then what's the matter?"

More silence.

"Joseph?"

"Nothing's the matter," he says. But there is, because he sounds sad, just like at Chipotle when he couldn't burp. When he asked if everyone thought he was weird.

Oh.

Puzzle pieces come together in my mind.

Burping, knuckle-cracking, fractions. Not knowing about Lester. Things change and life goes on and it's not always easy, that's what Mom said, and I guess that's especially true for Joseph. I guess I haven't thought about that as much as I should have.

And Mr. Marconi, he's a whole 'nother piece of the puzzle because of how he's always trying to escape from the nursing home. He keeps trying to go back to the way his life used to be, but it's never going to happen.

And then . . . me. I'm a puzzle piece, too. Ever since Joseph came back to school, all I've wanted is for us to be best friends again, in the plain old Joseph-and-Ty way and without so many other people butting in. *That's* what I wanted Joseph to understand. *That's* what I wanted Joseph to agree with.

All of that is true. All of that makes up part of the picture. I think there's a puzzle piece I've been missing, though.

When Joseph was absent from school for all those months, the rest of us kept going. Then Joseph came back, and I guess things felt really different to him. I guess he felt like he missed out on a lot of stuff, which he did. I guess he felt left behind, which he kind of was.

For me, things felt different, too, but I was Mr. Marconi. I wanted to go back in time when all Joseph wanted was to go forward.

The earth spins, and I fall back against my pillow. Of course Joseph wants to go forward. It makes sense to me now, but I feel pretty stupid.

"Can I call you back?" I ask Joseph.

"Um . . . sure?"

"Okay, great. Bye."

I push the end call button and hold the phone on my chest. I stare at the ceiling. I haven't done a great job of being Joseph's friend this week. Like how I felt left out because he was the sun and I was space junk. Whatever! I bet he never *felt* like the sun. I bet *he* even felt like space junk, sometimes!

It takes a while to straighten out my feelings

inside me. But once I do, I lift the phone and punch in Joseph's number.

"I have an idea," I say after he answers.

"You do?"

"Yeah. Do you want to know what it is?"

"Um, sure."

"Both," I say. "We could do both."

"Huh?"

"What we were talking about! Sometimes it could be just you and me, but other times we could do stuff with everyone. Well, maybe not Taylor. Or maybe Taylor. We could decide on the day of." I take a breath. "What do you think?"

I'm nervous, but Joseph doesn't make me wait for long.

"I think yes!" he says.

"Yay!"

I can hear how happy he is, and I'm happy, too. I feel happier than I've felt all week. And who knows? Playing with John and Chase and the others might be fun. It probably will be, with Joseph as part of the group.

Now that I've figured things out, I'm ready to move on.

"Are we going to tell Lexie about catching Fernando?" I ask.

"She'll never believe us," Joseph says.

"If we both tell her, she'll have to." My chest feels looser. I feel more like *me*. "I agree that she'll be all *nuh-uh* about it, though."

"We need to figure out how to catch her unawares," Joseph says.

"A bird ambush!" I say. "Only without birds!"

"'No birds were harmed in this ambush,'" Joseph says in a TV commercial voice.

I laugh. I settle into the fort of pillows and stuffed animals on my bed and wiggle around till I'm good and comfortable. "So. What, exactly, is our plan?"

CHAPTER TEN

On Friday, before morning meeting, Joseph gives me a Ziploc bag of chocolate-covered potato chips.

"Thanks!" I say. I'd forgotten about those chocolate-covered potato chips.

"I'd hide them if I were you," Joseph says in a spy voice. He gestures at Chase, who is playing paper football with John, and at Hannah and Elizabeth, who are making bracelets in the crafts area. "If you don't, everyone's going to want one."

"Smart," I say. "Oh, and here." I hand him his red hat.

"Thanks." He looks at it, and I wonder if he's thinking what I'm thinking, which is that here he is, not wearing his hat, and no one has said a thing.

He puts his hat in his desk. *Cool beanie-weenies,* I think. That leads to me thinking, *Cool benis-weenises,* but no, that is not a good think about, because what if I accidentally say it out loud?

We have eleven minutes of free choice before the day officially starts. Maybe more, because every so often Mrs. Webber comes in late. One morning I saw her in the teacher's lounge with Mr. Glasgow, the other second-grade teacher. They had Starbucks cups in their hands, and they were both off topic since they were talking to each other instead of teaching their classes.

But Joseph and I have at least eleven minutes to sneak-attack Lexie and tell her about Fernando while she's putting her stuff in her cubby. We want to tell her first off, because lots of mornings she has drowsy eyes when she first gets to school. Sometimes she shows up with a bump in her ponytail, which means she slept too late and had to hurry to get ready for the day.

I know about bumps in ponytails because of
Winnie and Sandra. Neither of them would allow
a bump to live in her ponytail, never-not-ever.

Joseph grabs my arm. "She's coming. She's
coming!"

I glance at the door. She is! She doesn't have
drowsy eyes, but she does have the last bite of a
Pop-Tart in her hand. That means she had to eat
breakfast on the run. That's a good sign.

"Hi, Lexie," Joseph says.

"Hi, Ty," I say. I whack my forehead. "I mean,
hi, Lexie!"

Joseph laughs, because we just started and
already I've messed up. *Not* cool benis-weenises!

"You don't know your own name?" Lexie says,
eating the final crusty part of her Pop-Tart. She
throws the foil wrapper in the trash. "Go back to
first grade."

"I know *my* name, just not *yours*." Joseph and I
go to her cubby.

"Guess what?" Joseph says.

"What?"

"Ty and I caught a bird yesterday."

Other kids' ears prick up, probably because of the bird-catching recitation I did last week.

"What kind of bird?" Lexie says. She turns from her cubby. "A stuffed bird?"

Elizabeth comes closer. So do Chase and Taylor and Breezie. No one says anything about Joseph not wearing his hat, and I'm proud of them. Maybe they don't even notice, but still.

"Nope," I say. "A *real* bird, with real feathers and a real beak and a real heart that beat super fast."

"Did you really?" Chase says, while at the same time, Lexie says, "You did not."

"They might have," Breezie says. "You don't know everything, Lexie."

Which means that Breezie is still mad at Lexie. *Hmm.* Too bad they didn't have a working-it-out like Joseph and I did.

Lexie folds her arms over her chest. "Where is it, then? Did you bring it to school?"

"Why would we bring a bird to school?" Joseph says.

"To feed to Lester!" Taylor say.

Everyone looks at him like, *Really, Taylor? Really?*

"We didn't bring him to school, and we never would," I say. "Unless it was pet show-and-tell day. But, even so, we couldn't, because we had to let him go."

"Ha!" Lexie says. "You 'had' to let him go? Boo-hoo. Too bad, so sad."

"No, because he was sick. We rescued him, or he would have died. But now a veterinarian is taking care of him."

"When he's better, he'll be released back into the wild," Joseph says.

"Uh-huh," Lexie says. "Where's your proof?"

Joseph and I grin at each other. We hoped she'd ask that question. I take a piece of computer paper out of my back pocket and unfold it. Everyone crowds around.

"It *is* a bird!" Breezie exclaims.

"Why is the picture black-and-white?" Chase asks.

"I have a raccoon trap in my backpack," Taylor announces. He stands on his tiptoes at the outside of the circle, trying to see in. He moves from spot to spot. "I do. I'm not even kidding."

"My sister took a picture of him on her phone," I say. "She printed it for me on the printer."

"Why don't you have colored ink?" Chase says.

Lexie holds out her hand. I give her the picture. She glances at it, snorts, and gives it back. "Fake."

"What?" Joseph says.

Lexie sticks her nose up in the air. She is an expert at sticking up her nose. "Who says *your sister* took that picture? Who says it isn't just a random bird you found on the computer?"

"I do," I say.

"Can I see?" Breezie asks.

I pass the picture to her. She studies it for longer than Lexie did. She doesn't just skim her eyes over it.

"The bird's in a shoebox," Breezie says.

"Yeah," I say. "That was to keep him safe."

She lifts her head. "Ty, show me your arm."

I'm confused, but I stick out my arm.

"Your other arm."

I stick out my other arm.

Breezie nods and hands me back the picture. "It's a real bird, and Ty and Joseph really did catch it," she pronounces. "Because of the bracelet. See?"

Oh yeah! The rubber bracelet from Chipotle! When Winnie took the picture, I was holding the shoebox in my lap. *I'm* not in the picture, at least not my face, but my arms are. On my wrist is my blue rubber bracelet. The same blue rubber bracelet I'm wearing right now!

"I have one, too," Joseph says, thrusting out his arm.

"You're lucky," Breezie says. She touches it. "Can I have it?"

He wrinkles his brow. I guess he doesn't know what to do when girls ask for stuff, either.

"Um . . . sure?" he says. He wiggles it off and gives it to her.

"Aw," Elizabeth says. "You should have given it to me!"

"Or me," Lexie says. "But, I mean, never mind, because it's ugly. No offense."

Everyone starts jibber-jabbering.

Elizabeth says that saying "no offense" is rude, and Breezie agrees.

Chase tells everyone about his rubber bracelets. "I pretty much collect them," he says. "They all say different things, and the reason I'm not wearing them is because they get in the way when I try to write. But boys *are* allowed to wear that kind of bracelet."

Of course they are, I think, as Silas talks on top of Chase about his own rubber bracelet collection. Boys are allowed to wear any kind of bracelet they want to. Most just don't.

Hannah brings up her gymnastics class. She says that in gymnastics, jewelry isn't allowed, period. Natalia tells everyone that she just started piano lessons and that piano is harder than gymnastics.

Maybe it is or maybe it isn't, I think, but what happened to talking about Fernando? What happened to the Great Bird Capturing story Joseph and I were going to act out?

Oh well. Things change.

I realize I'm okay with it, which makes me feel grown up.

Mrs. Webber comes in and tells us all to settle down. Nobody listens. She tells us it's time for morning meeting. Nobody listens. She does the *clap-clap clap-clap-clap* rhythm that we're supposed to clap back at her, and Joseph and I look at each other, but since no one claps back, we don't, either.

"I don't want to smell your shoe, Taylor," John says. "If you ask me again, I'm going to give you a wedgie. I mean it."

Taylor gestures at his privates, which he shouldn't do, and says, "Hey! Leave my pee-pee out of this!"

I wander toward the front of the room, because I can't not listen to Mrs. Webber for very long. If I do, my stomach will start to hurt. Plus she's heading for the light switch, and I know what happens after the light is turned off and on.

I sit on the floor and think about Fernando. I hope Sam's helping him feel better.

I think about all the pets I tried to get for Baby Maggie, even though she didn't want any of them. I make a list of them in my head:

A monkey, a fly, a puppy. A hyena and a platypus.

A snake (like Lester), and a ferret and a hedgehog and a jackalope. An armadillo and a camel. Also a mouse, a koala bear, and a rabbit.

Wowzers. That is a lot of pets. If I had all of those pets, I'd have to build them a pet condominium, with different size rooms and places to eat and drink, and—ha—an emergency exit just in case. Maybe the ferret would escape. Maybe the ferret would dash into Sandra's room and hide in her fluffy Ugg boots, and she would never know it until she put her boots on and it bit her toe.

Joseph sits down next to me. We smile.

Mrs. Webber blinks the lights off and on. When that doesn't work, she threatens to get out the egg timer, and one by one the other kids come and sit down, too. I look at them, and it occurs to me that I do like them. Even though sometimes they're annoying.

I look at Joseph, who's saying "oh, cool" as Chase describes his rubber bracelets some more.

I look at Elizabeth, who's tugging a scowly faced Lexie to the front of the room. I look at Breezie, who's wearing Joseph's rubber bracelet. The bracelet doesn't seem very Breezie-ish, not with her pretty hair and her pretty dress. But maybe she doesn't always want to be Breezie-ish?

Taylor is still talking about his pee-pee. Mrs. Webber strides to her desk, grabs the egg timer, and goes up behind him. She puts her hands on his shoulders and steers him to the far corner of the room. She tells him he needs to take a time-out.

"Aw, man!" Taylor complains, but he sits down with a thud. The corner of the room is better than outside in the hall, though. The corner of the room is a good spot for him.

I'm happy inside my skin, and my heart swells, because we're all in spots that are good for us. We're all exactly where we need to be.

READ THE FIRST BOOK STARRING TY!

READ THE SECOND BOOK STARRING TY!